04813

PUFFIN BOOKS

EDDIE AND THE BAD EGG

Herbie Brennan is the author of more than sixty books for children and adults, including the best-selling *Grailquest* series. He and his wife live in Ireland, where their lives are ruled by a cat called The Maggot and five of his relations who keep all the ducks at a distance.

DUDLEY SCHOOLS
LIBRARY SERVICE

Schoo

D1392323

Herbie Brennan
Eddie and the
Bad Egg

Illustrated by Ann Kronheimer

PUFFIN BOOKS

For Jacks

PUFFIN BOOKS

Published by the Penguin Group
Penguin Books Ltd, 27 Wrights Lane, London W8 5TZ, England
Penguin Putnam Inc., 375 Hudson Street, New York, New York 10014, USA
Penguin Books Australia Ltd, Ringwood, Victoria, Australia
Penguin Books Canada Ltd, 10 Alcorn Avenue, Toronto, Ontario, Canada M4V 3B2
Penguin Books (NZ) Ltd, Private Bag 102902, NSMC, Auckland, New Zealand

On the World Wide Web at: www.penguin.com

Penguin Books Ltd, Registered Offices: Harmondsworth, Middlesex, England

First published 2000
1 3 5 7 9 10 8 6 4 2

Text copyright © Herbie Brennan, 2000
Illustrations copyright © Ann Kronheimer, 2000
All rights reserved

The moral right of the author and illustrator has been asserted

Printed in Hong Kong by Midas Printing Ltd

Except in the United States of America, this book is sold subject to the condition that
it shall not, by way of trade or otherwise, be lent, re-sold, hired out, or otherwise
circulated without the publisher's prior consent in any form of binding or cover other
than that in which it is published and without a similar condition including
this condition being imposed on the subsequent purchaser

British Library Cataloguing in Publication Data
A CIP catalogue record for this book is available from the British Library

ISBN 0–141–30165–1

DUDLEY PUBLIC LIBRARIES

L 45746

631299 | SCH

JJ

··· Contents ···

1. Chicken in the Soup

My name is Eddie. I'm a duck. I run a downtown ducktective agency.

It was a slow day at the office. But then there was a knock on my door.

"Come in," I called. That's what I do when somebody knocks.

The door opened. My girl,
Gloria, brought in a frozen chicken.

"Who's this?" I asked.

"Don't you recognize your cousin
Charlie?" growled the chicken.

I took off my shades so I could
see him better. "Charlie? Charlie

Chicken? You look awful."

"I'm just cold," Charlie shrugged.
"What happened to the heat in here?"

"Got cut off when I didn't pay
the bill," I told him.

"All ducks have bills," said
Charlie sympathetically.

I hauled my feet off the desk and waddled over to the filing cabinet.

I found a bottle under *B* and poured us both a shot of swamp water. "What brings you into town?" I asked.

"It's my boy Larry," Charlie said. "He's got himself mixed up with a bunch of gangsters."

It didn't surprise me. Even as a youngster Larry was a bad egg. But I said nothing.

Charlie sipped his swamp water. "They're planning to smuggle in some lowlife from South America. Small-time criminal calls himself Mr Big. If Larry gets caught, they'll lock him in a coop and throw away the key."

I sniffed, which is hard to do when you're a duck. "What do you want me to do about it?"

Charlie looked me straight in my beady eye. "Catch the gangsters," he said sourly. "And talk some sense into my boy Larry."

2. A Lead from the Lawyers

When Charlie left, I finished the swamp water and did a little thinking. I had to get a lead on the gangsters who had their hooks in Larry. So I called some lawyers I knew who specialized in gangsters.

"Grisham, Grisham, Grisham, and Grisham, Law Attorneys," the voice announced at the other end of the phone.

"Let me talk to Mr Grisham," I said.

"Mr Grisham's just gone out," the voice told me.

"In that case I'll speak with Mr Grisham," I said.

"Sorry, Mr Grisham's in a meeting."

"OK," I said, "put me through to Mr Grisham."

"I'm afraid Mr Grisham has flu."

I said, "Then maybe I could have a word with Mr Grisham."

"Speaking," said the voice.

"Eddie the Duck here, Grisham," I said quickly. "Know anything about a clown from South America calls himself Mr Big?"

"Sure thing, Eddie," said

Grisham. "Small-time crook with a big moustache. Real name's Tiny Little. Wanted by the police all over the world. Our contacts say a gang of bad guys are planning to bring him into the country to help them rob some banks."

"Know where?" I asked.

"Word has it they're using the old airfield on the East Side. Nobody goes there any more."

"Know when?" I asked.

"I hear it's midnight tonight," said Grisham, "but don't tell them I told you."

"Thanks, Grisham, I owe you one," I said as I put down the phone.

I had this tight feeling in my

stomach, like somebody just mentioned green peas. If it was midnight tonight, I had to get my skates on. Fortunately, I kept them handy in a drawer. I tied the straps and reached for my best hat, the one that fitted.

I was halfway across town before I remembered I'd left my splurge gun in the desk.

3. Big Scoop

My plan was simple. I'd skate out to the old airport and have a look round before the bad guys arrived. Then I'd hide myself away somewhere I could see the plane come in.

Once I was sure they really were smuggling in Mr Big,

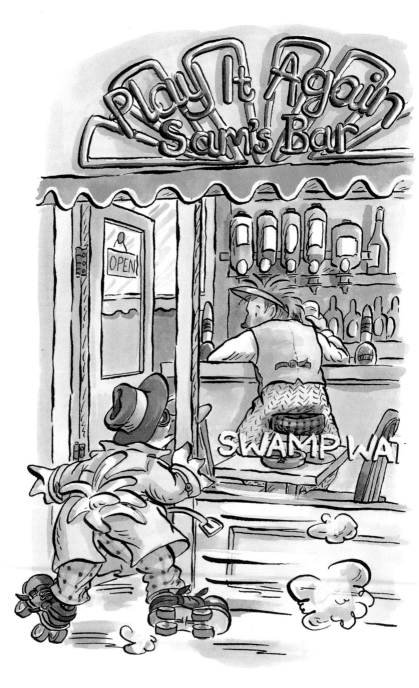

I'd make contact with Larry and warn him to get out of the way. Then I'd call the cops on my mobile and have everyone else picked up.

I figured when Larry saw the bad guys arrested, it would make him think twice about joining the gang.

There was only one problem. I didn't know what Mr Big looked like. That meant I had to pay a quick call on my old pal Scoop Figs of the *Daily Clarion*.

I found him at Play It Again Sam's Bar.

"Hi, Eddie – want a shot of swamp water?" he called out when he saw me.

"No time, Scoop," I told him. "I need a photograph of Mr Big."

Scoop frowned. "What's his real name?"

"Mr Little," I said.

Scoop's frown got deeper. "Mr Little? What's his first name?"

"Tiny."

"So Mr Big is Tiny Little?" Scoop asked.

"That's about the size of it."

"I think we've got his photo on file," Scoop said.

We went over to the *Clarion*. He walked, I skated. On the way, I told him what I knew about Mr Big being smuggled in.

I hung around reception until

Scoop came back with the picture. Mr Big looked bad all right. He might be Little, but he had a very big moustache. Looked like a dead rat under his nose. "I'd like to keep this," I told Scoop.

"No problem," Scoop said. "But do me a favour, would you?"

"Anything I can, Scoop," I said cheerfully.

Scoop looked at me. "Take care, Eddie. This guy's dangerous."

4. Dozy Duck

It had started to rain by the time I reached the edge of town. I took off my skates and hailed a cab.

"Nice day for ducks," the driver said as I climbed inside.

I ignored the funny. "Get me to the old airport," I snapped. "And don't take the scenic route."

"OK, duckie," he said. "Keep your down on."

I sank back in the seat and stared through the window. It was still five hours away from midnight, but already it was getting dark. At this time of night the city has a thousand faces, none of them pretty,

a thousand stories, all of them
scary. But it was still my city.

Rush hour traffic hadn't all died
down, so it was a long run out of
town, but we got to the old airport
at last. It hadn't been used since the
new one was built on the North
Side. Now all that was left were

empty, crumbling buildings, cracked concrete runways and notices that said *KEEP OUT*. The cab pulled up beside one of them.

"Far as I go, buddy," he said. "This place gives me the creeps."

I watched him drive off, then ducked inside.

There were seven runways, but six of them were too broken up now for planes to land. That meant if Mr Big was coming in at all, it had to be the seventh.

I looked around for somewhere to use as a lookout. The old control tower stood up like a broken tooth. That had to be the place.

It was gloomy inside, but the airport security lights shone through the broken windows so I had enough light to see my way.

I climbed a spiral staircase up to a big room where they used to watch the planes and tell them when to land. You could see the whole of the seventh runway from there. It was perfect.

There were still four hours left to midnight. I figured the bad guys

might come sooner, but even so, I had a lot of time to kill. I squatted near the big window, pulled my hat down over my eyes and figured to catch forty winks.

Minutes later, I was fast asleep.

5. Duck for Dinner

The big guy stuck a splurge gun in my ear. "Freeze, turkey!" he growled.

I sat up with a start. "I'm not a turkey – I'm a duck!" I said. But he wasn't listening.

"How come you're spying on us,

turkey? What are you? Some sort of cop?" he asked.

It was no good lying. "I'm a private ducktective," I said. "That's a private eye to you."

The big guy sniffed. "So you're a private duckeye? Know what we do with private duckeyes round here?" He pushed his face close to mine. His breath smelled like he'd swallowed a wet dog.

"No," I gulped.

He smiled. "We have them for dinner!"

I figured I wouldn't hang around to find out what he was planning for dessert. Before he could pull the splurge gun trigger, I was up and running.

I made it outside without too much trouble, but next thing I knew, the big guy had me cornered.

"How did you do that?" I blinked.

He smiled coldly. "You were running round in circles," he said.

Next minute, I was trussed up like a chicken and sitting on a plate. The big guy had been joined by eleven others. They were all waving knives and forks.

One held up a steaming jug. "Care for a little gravy, duck?" he asked.

6. Duck on the Lookout

I jerked awake, my heart pounding. What a nightmare that was!

I stood up to stretch my webs.

There was a sound from somewhere down below.

Quickly I crept to the window. This time it was no dream.

There were a dozen big guys with splurge guns on the runway.

I glanced at my watch. The luminous numbers showed eleven fifty-five so I figured it was five to midnight. I'd been asleep for hours. But that didn't matter. I was awake now. Mr Big would be arriving in five minutes.

I checked my pockets. I had the picture Scoop gave me. I had my mobile to call the cops. But at the back of my mind I kept thinking something was missing.

The big guys down below started to move forward as if they'd heard something and one looked up at the window where I was standing. I ducked back fast.

Then it hit me what was missing. There was no sign of Charlie Chicken's boy, Larry.

I wondered what it meant. Maybe he'd decided not to join the gang after all. Maybe they'd thrown him out. Maybe he was doing something for them somewhere else. Either way, it made things easier for me. If Larry wasn't here, I didn't

need to warn him. All I had to do
was call the cops and have these
goons run in.

But first I had to make sure Mr
Big was down safely.

As if in answer to my thoughts, I
heard the sound of a distant plane.

I waited.

The sound came closer. It had to
be Mr Big.

I moved back to the window and searched the sky for aircraft lights. I didn't hear a thing until the big guy stuck a splurge gun in my ear.

"Freeze, turkey!" he growled.

"I'm not a turkey – I'm a duck!" I sighed. But he still wasn't listening.

7. Dizzy Duck

They never expect you to fly.
I exploded in a cloud of
feathers and was up above the big
guy's head before he could even
think of pulling the trigger.

I dropped down behind him
and ran flat out for the spiral
staircase.

I slid down the banister to save time. Boy, was that a mistake! By the time I reached the bottom, the world was spinning round me. I tried to run, but hit a wall. Tweetie birds started singing in my head.

I turned round, balanced on one leg. The big guy was racing towards me. I could see the door that would get me out of here, but it wouldn't stand still.

I ran seven steps forward, turned and fell on my face. The ground was spinning so I spread my wings to keep a grip. I could hear the big guy getting closer, but there wasn't much I could do about it.

Since my wings were spread, I flapped them. I was too dizzy to fly,

but it got me on my feet. The big
guy was only metres away. I figured
I'd surprise him and hurled myself
between his legs.

Somehow I collided with a pillar
holding up the ceiling. Then I hit the
floor again. Fortunately, it had
stopped spinning. Unfortunately, the

big guy had caught up with me.

"Oh no you don't, duck!" he grinned as he lifted me up by the collar.

"Freeze, turkey!" growled a voice behind us.

"I'm not a turkey – I'm a duck!" I groaned.

But the voice wasn't talking to me. When I looked round I saw my old friend Scoop Figs. He had a splurge gun pointed at the big guy's head.

8. Flattened Duck

The big guy set me down carefully and dusted off the shoulders of my trench coat. Then he put his hands up.

"What are you doing here, Scoop?" I asked.

"Followed you," said Scoop.

"Think I was going to miss a good story?"

"Where did you get the splurge gun?"

"Your office," said Scoop. "Gloria sent it over by courier. Said you'd left it behind." He tossed it over. "I think Mr Big has arrived. A plane touched down while you were playing tag with this guy."

I looked out the window while keeping one eye on the big guy.

You can do stuff like that when you're a duck. Scoop was right. A small plane had touched down and the moustache climbing out of it was Mr Big. I had them dead to rights.

"Help me tie this guy up," I said to Scoop. "Then I have a phone call to make."

The big guy was good as gold. We tied his hands behind his back with his belt and gagged him with a handkerchief.

I looked out the window again. The plane was still there, but there was no sign of Mr Big and the gang. They had to be about the airport somewhere, but I didn't have much time to lose.

I needed to make that call to the cops.

I dragged the mobile from my pocket and punched *ON*. The little screen lit up and I read what it said with a sinking heart: *BATTERY FLAT* .

9. Dead Duck

I did what any duck does when his phone won't work. I threw it on the ground and jumped on it. Then I picked it up and tried again.

"Freeze, turkey!" growled a voice behind me.

"He's not a turkey – he's a duck!" Scoop put in quickly.

I didn't figure it would do much
good.

I turned my head. Mr Big was
pointing a splurge gun at it. So was
every one of the eleven bad guys

who'd been outside to meet him.

Mr Big smiled a wicked smile. "Turkey . . . duck," he shrugged. "What's the difference? Where I come from we eat these birds for breakfast."

Most I can face is a cup of coffee, but I didn't let it get to me. "Mr Big, I presume?" I said. "Or should I call you Little?"

One of the bad guys fired a splurge above my head. "Cut the wisequacks, duck!" he warned. He came across and took away my splurge gun.

"Let him talk," said Mr Big easily. "What harm can he do? His phone's broke, we got his gun, there's no way he can get out."

He was right. I couldn't think of a thing to say.

The bad guys untied the big guy we'd tied up, then used his belt to tie up Scoop. I looked around desperately, but the splurge guns pointing my way never wavered. Mr Big watched with a big smug smile across his face. "This is one time the good guys lose," he sneered.

It looked like I was a dead duck.

10. Frozen Turkey

"Freeze, turkey!" growled a voice behind me.

"He's not a turkey – he's a duck!" everybody shouted.

"This is getting silly!" I groaned. But I turned round to a big surprise. Charlie Chicken's boy, Larry, was standing behind me holding a

double-barrelled Mark Four
automatic splurge gun and it wasn't
pointing at my head. He had it
aimed at Mr Big.

"Drop the guns, guys," he said.

I looked at Mr Big, then back at
Larry. "I thought you two were on
the same side," I frowned.

"So did my father," said Larry. "But I was never really with the bad guys. I've been working undercover for the FBI. They figured nobody would suspect a chicken."

Suddenly the big guy made a break for it. He only got halfway to the door. Without his belt,

his trousers fell down and he tripped. Larry swung the Mark Four to cover him and that gave Mr Big his chance.

He travelled fast for somebody carrying a heavy moustache. He was out the door before anyone could move.

"After him, Eddie!" Larry shouted. "I'll keep these goons covered!"

I grabbed my splurge gun from the guy who took it and headed after Mr Big. By the time I reached the open air, he was climbing into the cockpit of the little plane. It began to taxi down the runway, then took off. "You'll never catch me now!" he called.

But he forgot who he was talking
to. I did a running take-off and
landed on the wing. I stuck my gun
through the cockpit window.

"Freeze, turkey!" I said.